BUBBE ISABELLA
AND THE SUKKOT CAKE

This **PJ BOOK** belongs to

_____

_____

PJ Library®

JEWISH BEDTIME STORIES and SONGS

KELLY TERWILLIGER

PICTURES BY PHYLLIS HORNUNG

KAR-BEN
PUBLISHING

To my grandmother, Marjorie Isabel—K.T.

For the Peacocks—Roger, Jane, and Curtis—P.H.

Sukkot is a fall harvest holiday during which Jewish people recall how they wandered in the desert, dwelling in huts, after the exodus from Egypt. Some Jewish families build sukkot, temporary booths, decorated with branches and fruit. It is traditional to eat in the sukkah during the holiday. The week-long celebration culminates in another holiday, Simchat Torah. Each year in the synagogue the Torah (Five Books of Moses) is read from start to finish. On Simchat Torah, the last verses are read, and the cycle begins again. As the Torah scrolls are paraded around the synagogue, families dance, sing, and wave colorful flags.

Text copyright © 2005 by Kelly Terwilliger
Illustrations copyright © 2005 by Phyllis Hornung

Kar-Ben Publishing, Inc.
A division of Lerner Publishing Group
241 First Avenue North
Minneapolis, MN 55401 U.S.A.
1-800-4-KARBEN
Website address: www.karben.com

Library of Congress Cataloging-in-Publication Data
Terwilliger, Kelly, 1967–
      Bubbe Isabella and the Sukkot cake / by Kelly Terwilliger ; illustrations by Phyllis Hornung.
          p.   cm.
      Summary: Bubbe Isabella invites many animal guests to spend Sukkot with her, but they are more interested in eating the Sukkah than her lovely lemon cake.
      ISBN–13: 978–1–58013–187–2 (lib. bdg. : alk. paper)
      ISBN–10: 1–58013–187–5 (lib. bdg. : alk. paper)
      [1. Cake—Fiction. 2. Sukkah—Fiction. 3. Sukkot—Fiction. 4. Jews—Fiction.] I. Hornung, Phyllis, ill. II. Title.
PZ7.T2826Bu 2005
[E]—dc22   2004013502

Manufactured in China
3-43849-10227-3/13/2017

091721K4/B1084/A3

Bubbe Isabella picked two tomatoes and a
cucumber, the last of the vegetables in her garden.
"It's time to celebrate the end of the harvest," she said
to herself. So Bubbe Isabella decided to build a sukkah.
It had a grass floor, a roof of branches and leaves,
and three walls made from an old garden fence.

On the three walls she hung three pieces of colored cloth: yellow for sunshine, green for rain, and blue for the beautiful sky.

From the branches of her roof she hung apples and grapes, ears of corn, and tiny golden pumpkins.

Inside, she set a little table and two little chairs, and on the table she placed a freshly-baked lemon cake.

"Ah!" she sighed as she sat in her sukkah at last, listening to leaves rustle and crickets sing. "How lovely it is to sit in a sukkah and wait for the stars to wink awake. Now if only I had somebody to share this cake with me!"

She sang a welcoming song. Nobody knocked on her garden fence wall. But down at her feet, something caught her eye.

A fuzzy caterpillar crept along the grassy floor.

"Hello, Mr. Caterpillar!" said Bubbe Isabella.
"Would you like some lovely lemon Sukkot cake?"
"No, thank you," squeaked the caterpillar. "I don't
eat cake. Grass has always been best for me."

"Well, by all means, help yourself!" said Bubbe Isabella, and the caterpillar did. He munched his way across the floor, and they stayed up together telling jokes and singing songs until the sky was full of stars.

The next night when Bubbe Isabella
went into her sukkah, there was the
fuzzy caterpillar, waiting for her! But she
still had no one to share that cake. So
Bubbe Isabella sang her welcoming song
again. This time she saw a flicker of
wings overhead. She looked up. A moth!

"Good evening, Madam Moth," said Bubbe Isabella. "Would you like a piece of cake?"

"No, thank you," said the moth. "I don't eat cake. But I wouldn't mind sipping at your juicy grapes!"

"Please do!" said Bubbe Isabella, and she and the moth and the fuzzy caterpillar stayed in the sukkah telling jokes and singing songs until the sky was full of stars.

The next night, Bubbe Isabella joined the moth and the fuzzy caterpillar and sang her welcoming song again. "Surely," she said, "there is someone out there who would like to eat some cake with me!" There was a rustle in the trees and down hopped a squirrel.

"Oh, Mr. Squirrel!" cried Bubbe Isabella. "Would you like a piece of cake?"

"No, thank you, I don't eat cake," said the squirrel. "But I do like corn!"

"Well then, please help yourself," said Bubbe Isabella. The squirrel scampered up onto her leafy roof and began to nibble at an ear of corn. Bubbe Isabella, the squirrel, the moth, and the fuzzy caterpillar stayed in the sukkah telling jokes and singing songs until the sky was full of stars.

The next night who should come when
Bubbe Isabella sang her song but a raccoon.
He did not want cake, but he munched away
on apples, and they all stayed up together
telling jokes and singing songs until the sky
was full of stars.

The next night, a deer arrived and looked so
longingly at the leafy roof that Bubbe Isabella let
her eat it. The night after that, a porcupine waddled
up and gnawed happily on the walls. Nobody wanted
cake, but they all stayed up together telling jokes
and singing songs until the sky was full of stars.

Bubbe Isabella's sukkah was growing rather shabby. Everything had been munched and nibbled except the golden pumpkins, the lemon cake, and the three pieces of colored cloth. But Bubbe Isabella didn't mind. She loved the company, and only wished that somebody would eat her lovely lemon Sukkot cake.

That night there was a loud shuffle and crunch from the trees, and a great big old bear lumbered up.

"Good evening, Mr. Bear! Would you like a piece of cake?" called Bubbe Isabella. But when the bear snuffled and stumbled up to the sukkah, he sat SPLAT! right on top of the lovely lemon cake.

"What yummy golden pumpkins you have here!" rumbled the bear, never noticing how sticky he was underneath.

"Please—do help yourself," said Bubbe Isabella, wiping frosting off her apron.

So the bear did, and they all stayed up together telling jokes and singing songs until the sky was full of stars.

The holidays were coming to a close. Bubbe Isabella's sukkah was tattered and bare. Everyone had gone, except for the caterpillar who lay curled asleep on a dry leaf. What a fine and happy place this had been! Bubbe Isabella thought she could smell rain in the air. Very quietly, she sang a welcoming song and carefully placed another dry leaf over the caterpillar so it wouldn't get wet.

Bubbe Isabella was just about to go inside when
who should come around the side of the house but
a small boy.

"How lovely!" cried Bubbe Isabella. "Another guest!
Oh dear, I wish I could offer you a piece of cake,
but I'm afraid it's all quite squashed!"

"That's all right," said the little boy. "I'm not hungry. I just need a flag for Simchat Torah. Do you have an extra flag anywhere?"

Bubbe Isabella looked around. All she had left were cake crumbs and her lovely colored cloths hanging from their poles on what was left of the old garden fence.

"You know," she said slowly,
"I think I might!" She lifted one cloth.
"Here," she said. "Yellow for sunshine!"
The little boy's face glowed as he
took the banner in one hand. Bubbe
Isabella raised the next one: "Green
for rain!" she said, and the boy took
this one in his other hand. Last of all,
Bubbe Isabella lifted the third cloth from the
side of the sukkah. "Blue for the beautiful sky!"
she said, and waved it in the air.

Then, together they
went down the hill to join
the holiday procession.